HERE COME

DREAMWORKS

THE CROODS

adapted by Maggie Testa

Ready-to-Read

Simon Spotlight

New York   London   Toronto   Sydney   New Delhi

SIMON SPOTLIGHT

An imprint of Simon & Schuster Children's Publishing Division
1230 Avenue of the Americas, New York, New York 10020
This Simon Spotlight edition November 2020

DreamWorks The Croods © 2013 DreamWorks Animation LLC. All Rights Reserved.

For information about special discounts for bulk purchases, please contact Simon & Schuster Special Sales at
1-866-506-1949 or business@simonandschuster.com.
Manufactured in the United States of America 0920 LAK
2 4 6 8 10 9 7 5 3 1
ISBN 978-1-5344-6685-2 (pbk)
ISBN 978-1-5344-6686-9 (hc)
ISBN 978-1-5344-6687-6 (eBook)

Meet the Croods.
They are cavemen,
but they won't be for much longer.
Their world is about to change.

This is Grug.
Grug is the leader of the Croods.
He lives by three rules:
Anything new is bad.
Curiosity is bad.
Going out at night is bad.
He tells his family
to never not be afraid.

Grug is very strong,
and he loves his family very much.
He will do anything to keep them
safe.

This is Eep.
She is Grug's oldest daughter.
She doesn't like her father's rules.
She wants to meet new people,
see new sights,
and go on new adventures.

Grug reminds her that
anything new is bad.

When their cave collapses,
the Croods are forced to journey
into a whole new world.
Eep is excited.
So is her younger brother, Thunk.

Thunk wants to be strong,
just like his dad.
He is always eager to hunt
or help or chow down!
He just doesn't like it when
Gran tries to chow down on him!

This New World is filled
with new creatures.
Some of them look cute,
like fuzzy, little Bear Pears.

And some of them are dangerous,
like Punch Monkeys.
When Grug first encounters
a group of Punch Monkeys,
they hit him back and forth, as if
he's a pinball in a pinball machine!

And some creatures are just plain scary, like Piranhakeets.

A swarm of them can eat an entire Land Whale in a matter of seconds!

The Croods discover new things everywhere in this New World. They don't always know what to do.

Eep decides it's time to call someone who can help.

Who does she call? Guy!
When the Croods meet Guy,
he is living by himself.
He survives by inventing things
that help him stay safe . . .

. . . like a belt to hold his pants up, shoes to walk across spiky coral, and fire to cook food and scare dangerous creatures.

Grug doesn't think the family needs Guy's help. But Gran reminds him that they need his fire.

Grug agrees to bring him along on the Croods' journey.

Gran is the oldest Crood.
She wears a dress made out of
a lizard's skin.
The dress has a tail!

Gran is not a big fan of baths. She doesn't like losing her protective layer of dirt and bugs. She is also not a big fan of Grug, but deep down she loves him.

Grug's wife is Ugga.
Ugga always has her hands full
taking care of Sandy.

Sandy is the youngest Crood.
She is always running everywhere
and getting into everything!
She might be little, but she's
fearless.

As the Croods continue
on their journey to find a new cave
on the Mountain,
they see many more things
that are new to them . . .

. . . like popcorn.
At first, Grug doesn't want
his family to eat the popcorn
because it's new.
But they do, and it's delicious!

The Croods also learn new things.
Guy teaches them how to construct
a trap to catch a Turkeyfish.
Guy and Eep lure the Turkeyfish
into the trap with a puppet.
The Croods learn that cooked
Turkeyfish tastes better than
raw bugs.

When the Croods finally make it
to the Mountain, it starts to crumble!
Everyone wants to hide
in a cave for safety . . .
everyone except Grug.
He has changed.
He doesn't want his family to be
afraid of new things anymore.

He tells them to follow the light.
And they do!
Grug uses his strength
and his new ideas to help
him and his family get to
the other side of the Mountain.

Now the Croods live on the Beach,
where they can enjoy tomorrow.